D0471131

BATMAN ™ ETERNAL ENEMIES

BY JOHN SAZAKLIS
ILLUSTRATED BY ANDIE TONG

BATMAN created by Bob Kane

HARPER FESTIVAL
An Imprint of HarperCollinsPublishers

THE VILLAINS AND HEROES IN THIS BOOK!

RĀ'S AL GHŪL

The ruthless leader of the League of Assassins, Rā's al Ghūl's name literally translates to "Demon's Head." He is rumored to be hundreds of years old. To sustain immortality, the criminal mastermind bathes in mystical pools known as Lazarus Pits. His goal is to save the Earth from ecological devastation.

TALIA AL GHŪL

The daughter of Rā's al Ghūl, she is the second-in-command and heir of his evil empire. Trained from a young age in hand-to-hand combat and the use of most weapons, Talia is as deadly as she is beautiful. Together with her bodyguard, Ubu, she fights for her father's skewed dream of utopia.

J L.
Dic
BATMAN nb
faves

HarperFestival is an imprint of HarperCollins Publishers.

Eternal Enemies
Copyright © 2014 DC Comics.
BATMAN and all related characters and elements are trademarks of and © DC Comics.
(s14)
HARP30051

Manufactured in China.
No part of this book may be used or reproduced in any manner whatsoever without written permission except in the case of brief quotations embodied in critical articles and reviews.
For information address HarperCollins Children's Books, a division of HarperCollins Publishers, 10 East 53rd Street, New York, NY 10022.
www.harpercollinschildrens.com

Library of Congress catalog card number: 2013940682
ISBN 978-0-06-220997-9

13 14 15 16 17 SCP 10 9 8 7 6 5 4 3 2 1
❖
First Edition

BATMAN

After being orphaned as a child, young Bruce Wayne vowed to fight crime and injustice throughout Gotham City. He trained his body and mind to become Batman, the Caped Crusader! With his high-tech, crime-fighting gadgets and his armored vehicles, Batman fears no foe and is known as the World's Greatest Detective.

NIGHTWING

Dick Grayson, an orphaned acrobat, was adopted by Bruce Wayne and trained under Batman to become his sidekick, Robin. After Dick turned eighteen, he became Nightwing, the sole protector of the city Blüdhaven.

BATWOMAN

Kate Kane is an heiress from Gotham City. After she was rescued from a kidnapping attempt, Kate was inspired to follow in Batman's footsteps. Using her fortune to create her own crime-fighting hideout similar to the Batcave, she became the excellent martial artist, detective, and crime fighter known as Batwoman.

Billionaire Bruce Wayne and his friend Dick Grayson attend a charity benefit at the Gotham City Museum. Also present is the glamorous heiress Kate Kane. The three socialites gather around the museum's main attraction.

"The Scroll of Osiris," Bruce says. "It is the oldest Egyptian document ever found. Some say it contains ancient secrets of immortality."

Suddenly, glass shatters from the skylight above. A group of masked warriors drop in on the startled crowd. Bruce and Dick sneak out the back door, while Kate uses a side exit.

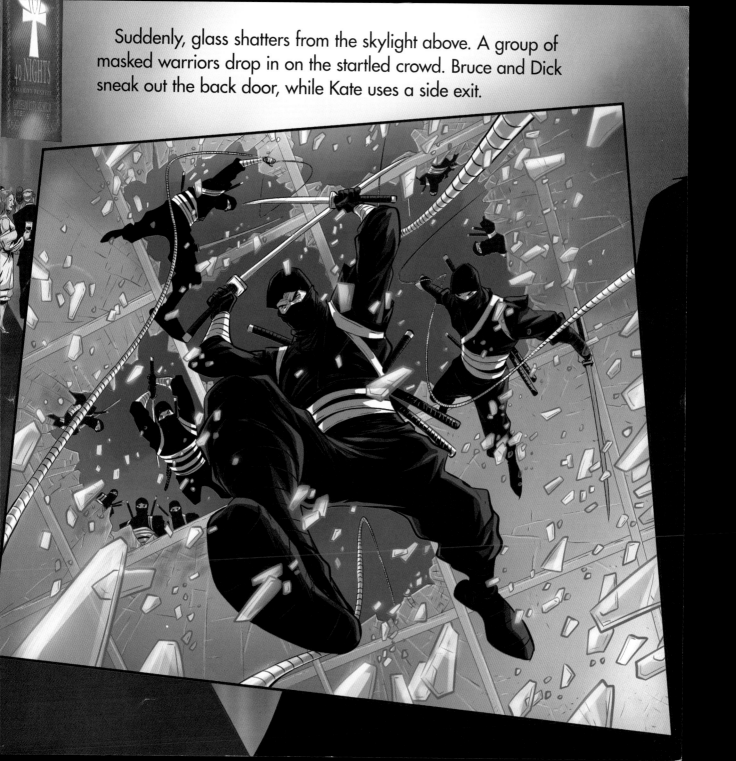

A severe man in ceremonial garb emerges from the pack. "Ladies and gentlemen, I am Rā's al Ghul," he says. "I hope you have eaten well, for the feast is now over."

Rā's approaches the display case. He smashes it with his fist and removes the priceless parchment.

The outer doors crash open to reveal Batman and Nightwing...
and an unexpected ally—Batwoman!
The super heroes rush at the thieves, but the henchmen hurl
exploding gas pellets. When the smoke clears, Rā's al Ghūl and his
followers are gone.

Moments later, the three heroes investigate the theft using Batman's mobile Batcomputer.

"Why would Rā's steal the Scroll of Osiris?" Nightwing asks.

"Osiris was the Egyptian god of the Underworld," Batwoman says. "He could grant life after death. Many have performed magic rituals in his honor in hopes of achieving eternal life."

"The scroll is really a map that leads to the ritual site," Batman says. "I believe it's also the location of a new Lazarus Pit."

"What's that?" asks Batwoman. Nightwing explains how the liquid in these mystical pools is an unknown chemical stew with restorative qualities.

"We must stop Rā's before he rejuvenates himself," Batman states. "The stronger he becomes, the harder he is to defeat!"

A few hours pass. Batman, Nightwing, and Batwoman are in the Batplane flying over Egypt. The tracking device the museum placed on the scroll shows that Rā's and his minions are headed for the Canyon of Tombs, a hidden sanctuary near Cairo.

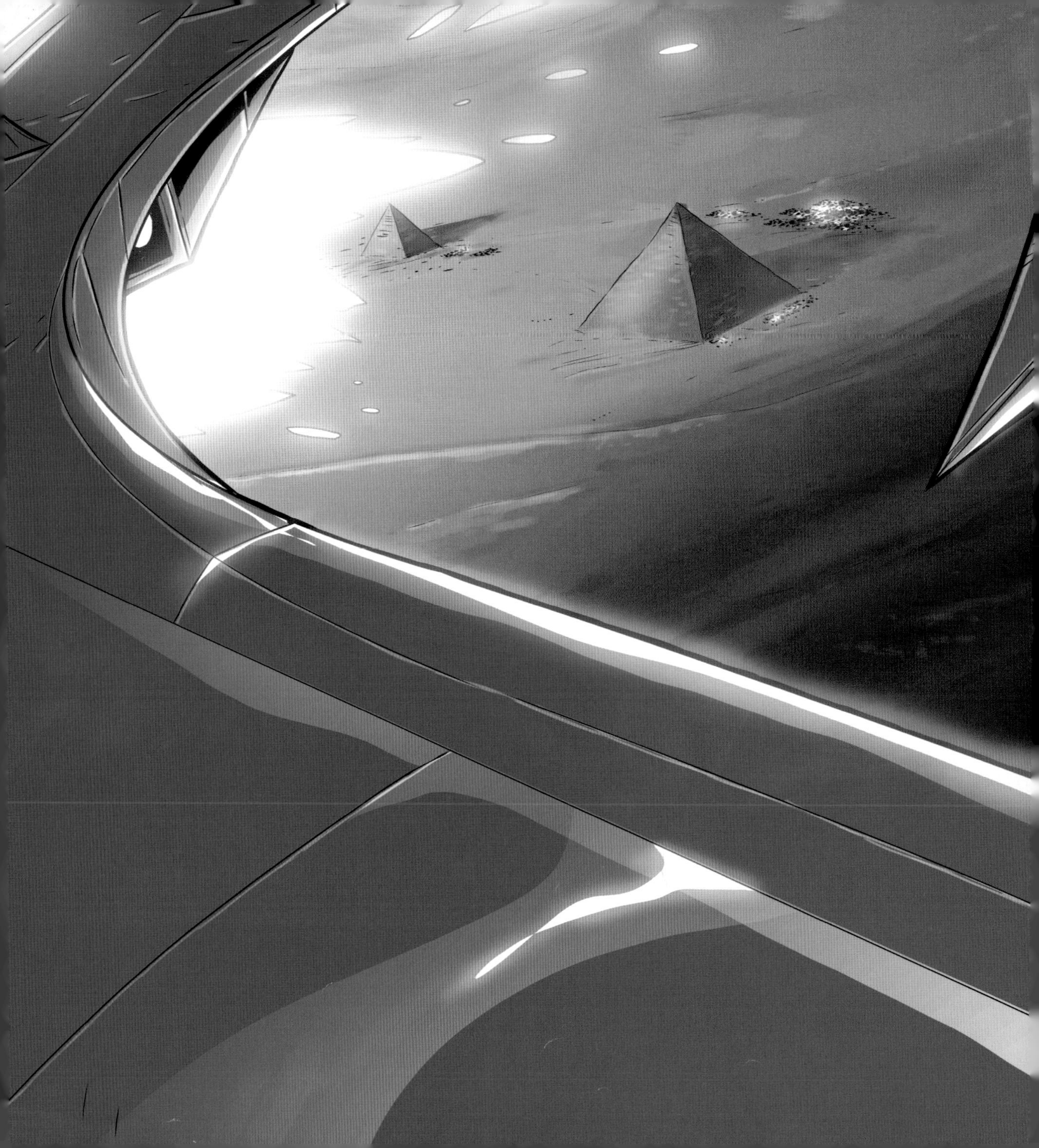

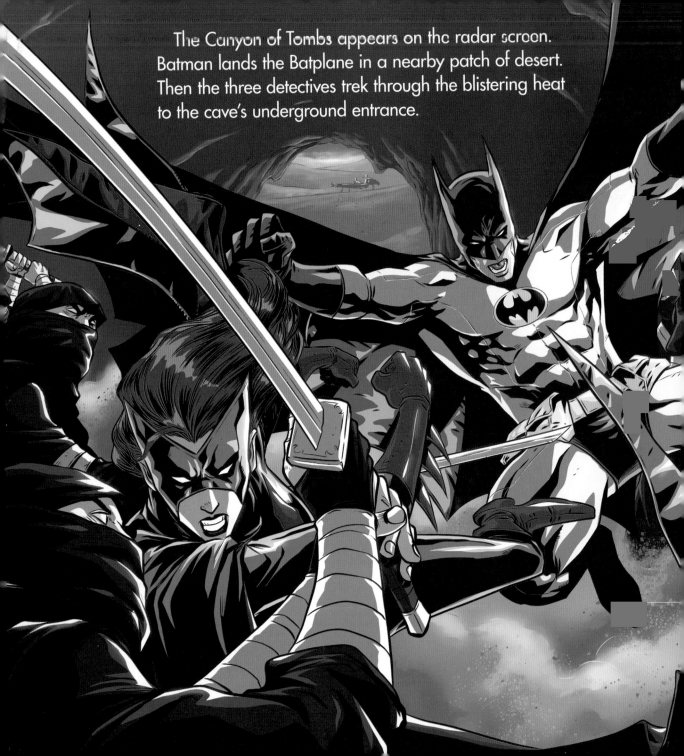

The Canyon of Tombs appears on the radar screen.
Batman lands the Batplane in a nearby patch of desert.
Then the three detectives trek through the blistering heat
to the cave's underground entrance.

After the heroes enter the cave, Rā's al Ghūl's henchmen immediately surround them.

"Looks like these guys don't want us playing in their sandbox," Nightwing quips. "The odds aren't so great, either."

"For *them*," Batwoman replies.

The League of Assassins strikes, but they are no match for this terrific trio!

Deep inside the excavation site, Rā's al Ghūl is with his beloved daughter, Talia, and their bodyguard, Ubu. They have discovered the new Lazarus Pit!

"This bubbling bath contains infinite knowledge and helps grant eternal life," Rā's says. "In a few short moments, I shall be revitalized!"

"Bath time is over," booms a deep voice. It's Batman! He and his friends have beaten Rā's' henchmen in time to interrupt the immortality ritual.

The Caped Crusader fires his grappling hook, ensnaring the villain, and pulls him away from the Pit.

"Eliminate them!" Rā's commands.

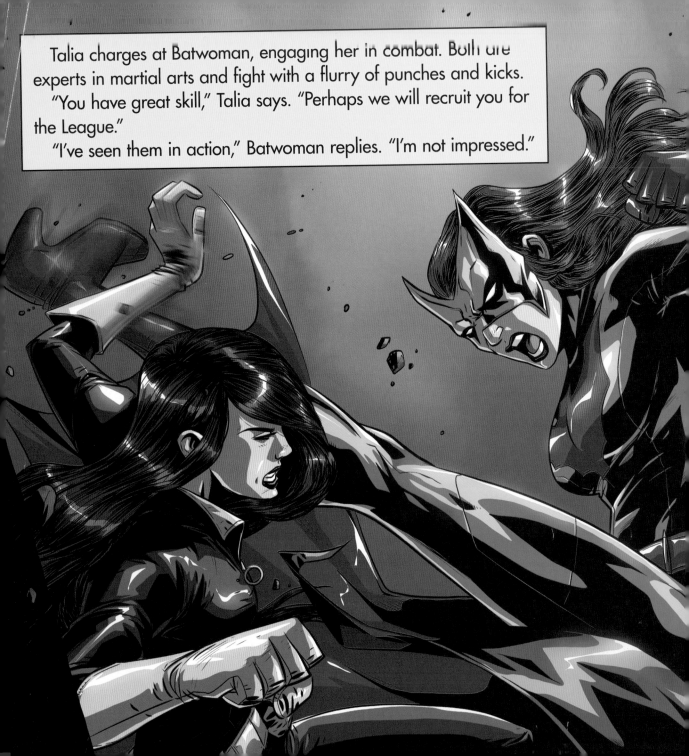

Talia charges at Batwoman, engaging her in combat. Both are experts in martial arts and fight with a flurry of punches and kicks.

"You have great skill," Talia says. "Perhaps we will recruit you for the League."

"I've seen them in action," Batwoman replies. "I'm not impressed."

Ubu rushes Nightwing, trying to pulverize him with his fists. The young hero expertly somersaults over a stone altar and lands on the muscle man's back. He grabs Ubu in a headlock. "The bigger they are, the more fun they are to fight!"

Meanwhile, Rā's al Ghūl unsheathes his weapon, the Serpent's Head, and slices through the Batrope. "For this indignity, I will make you suffer!" he yells, lunging at the Dark Knight.

Batman counters the attack with his lightning-fast reflexes.

"The League and I will cleanse the planet and start fresh," Rā's says as they battle. "This poor defiled world must be restored to its former glory!"

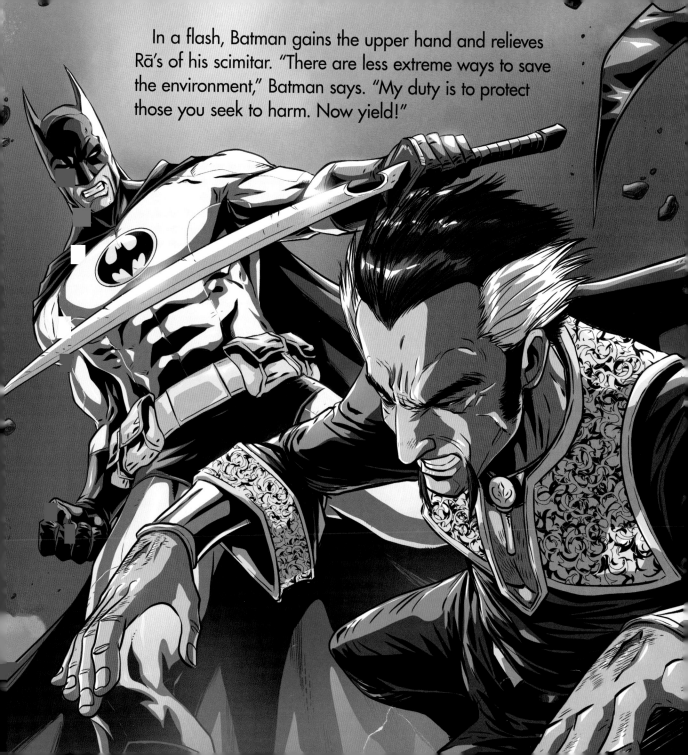

In a flash, Batman gains the upper hand and relieves Rā's of his scimitar. "There are less extreme ways to save the environment," Batman says. "My duty is to protect those you seek to harm. Now yield!"

Suddenly, the cavern walls begin to tremble and the ground shakes. The fighting has caused the fragile tomb walls to crack—they are starting to collapse!

"We need to get out of here!" Batman shouts. He grabs the Scroll of Osiris and puts it in his Utility Belt.

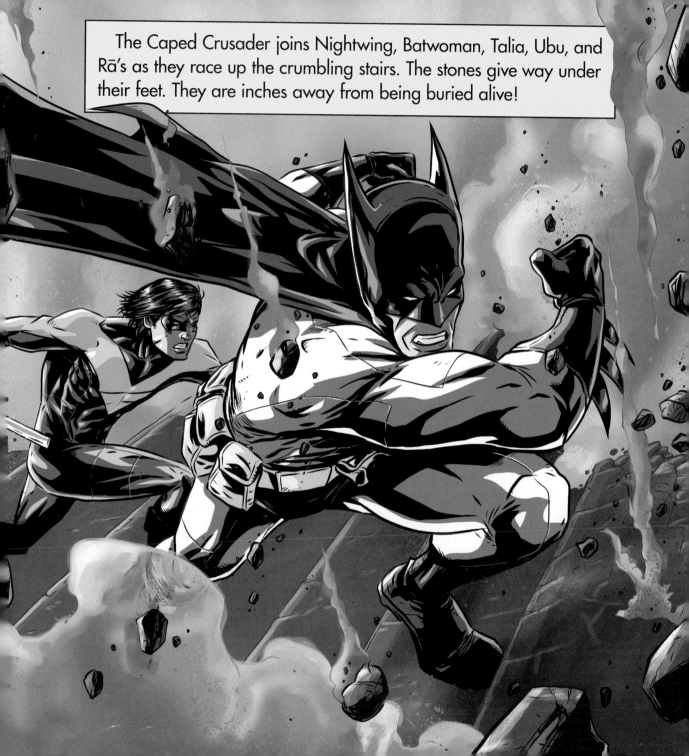

The Caped Crusader joins Nightwing, Batwoman, Talia, Ubu, and Rā's as they race up the crumbling stairs. The stones give way under their feet. They are inches away from being buried alive!

Everyone makes it safely to the surface, seconds before the walkway disappears. Rā's tumbles back, but Batman grabs him. The villain dangles in midair over the gaping chasm. "Help me save you," Batman grunts.

"Don't worry—this is only the beginning," Rā's al Ghūl replies calmly. "We shall meet again, Detective. . . ."

Rā's releases his grip and plummets into the waiting Lazarus Pit below.

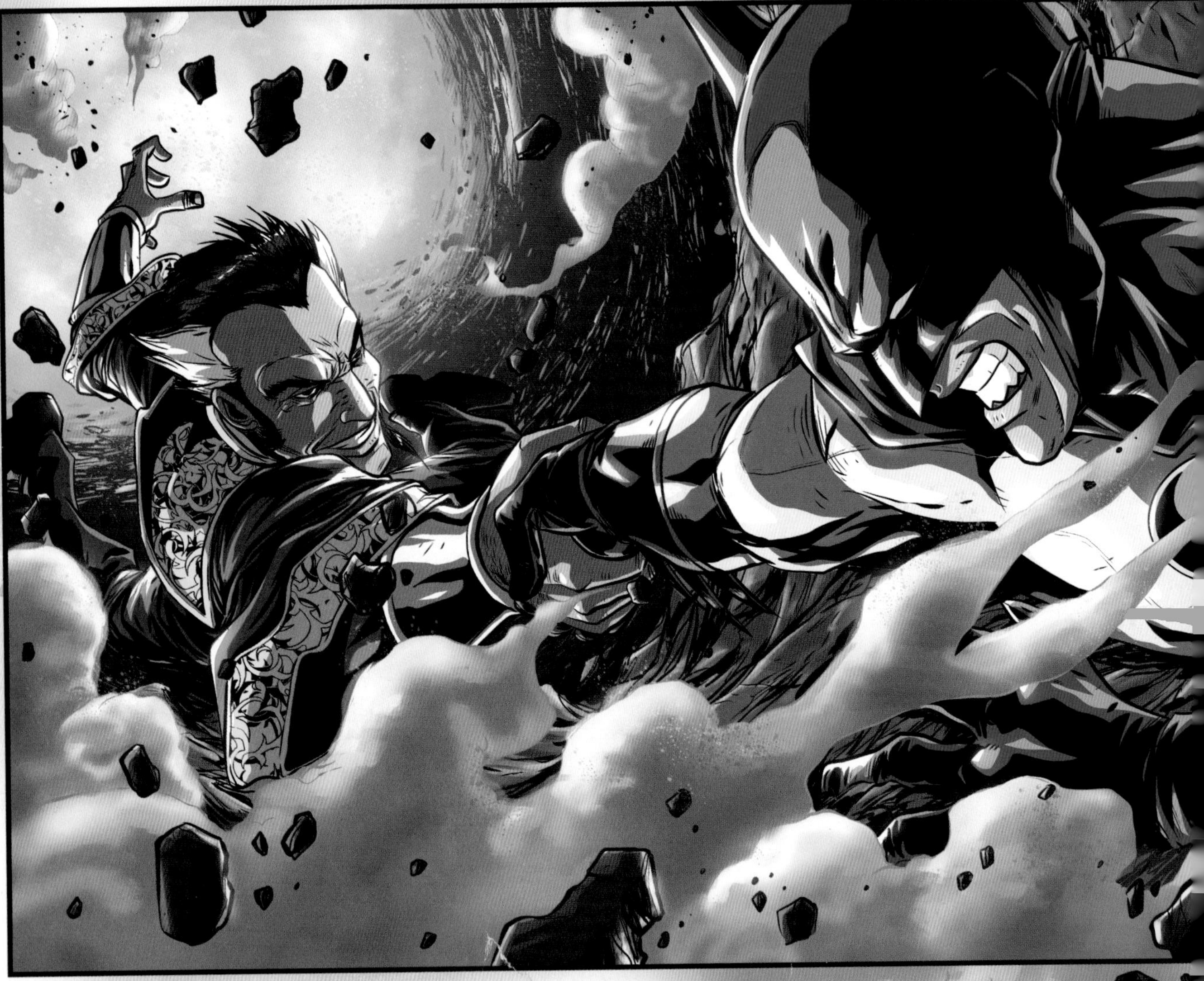

Nightwing and Batwoman handcuff Talia and Ubu and escort them silently to the Batplane.

Minutes later, the Batplane takes off, its course set for Gotham City. "You may have scattered the League, but this is a minor setback," Talia says. "We shall return with a vengeance. The League of Assassins will rise again!"

"And we will be ready to take you down again," Batman replies. "Until then, you and your friend can enjoy the hospitality of Blackgate Penitentiary."

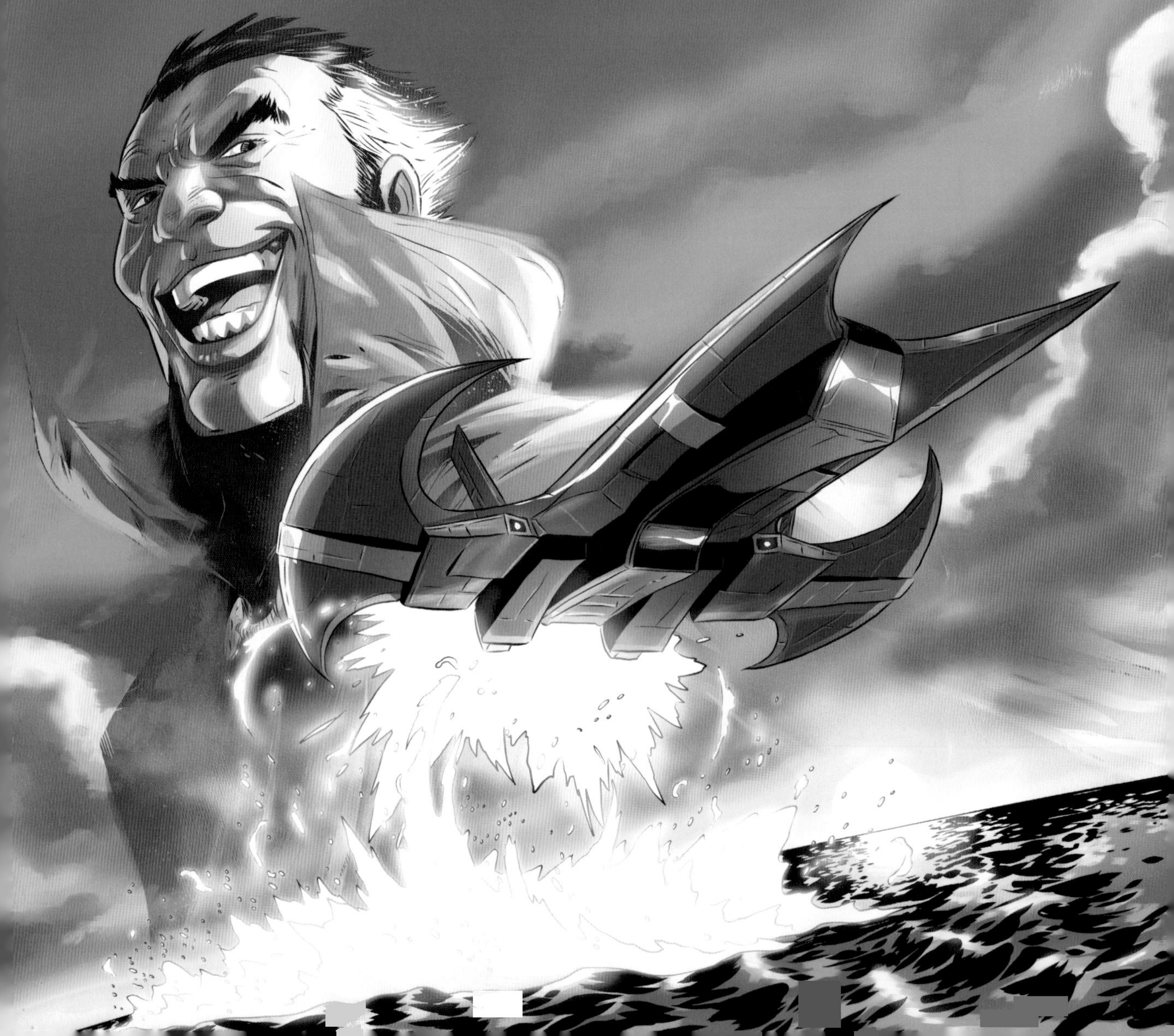